SKIDAMARINK

The "I LOVE YOU" Song

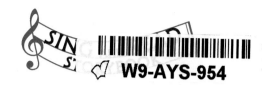

For Marcus, Dylan, and Ruby
— J.E.

ISBN 13: 978-0-439-89704-4

ISBN 10: 0-439-89704-1

12 11 10 9 8 7 6 5 9 10 11 12/0

Printed in the U.S.A. 23

First printing, January 2007

Book design by Janet Kusmierski

SING AND READ STORYBOOK™

SKIDAMARINK

The "I LOVE YOU" Song

Illustrated by Jacqueline East

SCHOLASTIC INC.
New York Toronto London Auckland Sydney
Mexico City New Delhi Hong Kong Buenos Aires

Skidamarink a dink a dink,

Skidamarink a doo,

I love you!

Skidamarink a dink a dink,

Skidamarink a doo,

I love you!

I love you in the morning

and in the afternoon,

I love you in the evening

and underneath the moon;

Oh, Skidamarink
a dink a dink,

Skidamarink a doo,

I love you!

I…love…YOU!

SKIDAMARINK
The "I LOVE YOU" Song

3
Skid - a - ma - rink - a dink - a dink
3
skid - a - ma - rink - a doo
I love you.
3
Skid - a - ma - rink - a dink - a dink
3
skid - a - ma - rink - a doo
I love you.